WIT

To the staff at King's College Hospital, London – real heroes

Special thanks to Brandon Robshaw

Bloomsbury Publishing, London, Berlin, New York and Sydney

First published in Great Britain in April 2012 by Bloomsbury Publishing Plc
50 Bedford Square, London, WC1B 3DP

A CIP catalogue record for this book is available from the British Library

ISBN 978 1 4088 1582 3

Typeset by Hewer Text UK Ltd, Edinburgh
Printed in Great Britain by Clays Ltd, St Ives Plc, Bungay, Suffolk

1 3 5 7 9 10 8 6 4 2

www.bloomsbury.com
www.starfighterbooks.com

MAX CHASE

BLOOMSBURY

LONDON BERLIN NEW YORK SYDNEY

UBI GALAXY

MEIGWOR SUN

MEIGWOR

ASTEROID FIELD

I.F. SPACE STATION

SUN

EARTH

MILKY WAY

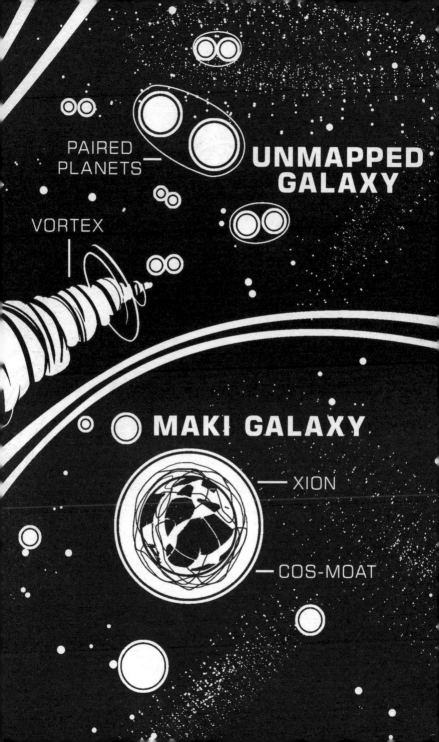

**An elite
fighting team sworn to protect and
defend the galaxy**

**It is the year 5012 and the Milky Way galaxy
is under attack . . .**

After the Universal War . . . a war that
almost brought about the destruction of
every known universe . . . the planets in the
Milky Way banded together to create the
Intergalactic Force – an elite fighting team
sworn to protect and defend the galaxy.

Only the brightest and most promising students are accepted into the Intergalactic Force Academy, and only the very best cadets reach the highest of their ranks and become . . .

To be a Star Fighter is to dedicate your life to one mission: *Peace in Space*. They are given the coolest weapons, the fastest spaceships – and the most dangerous missions. Everyone at the Intergalactic Force Academy wants to be a Star Fighter someday.

Do YOU have what it takes?

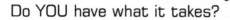

Chapter 1

Purple.

That was all Peri could see. He closed his eyes. He opened them again and turned 360 degrees. One moment they had been cruising in the *Phoenix*, watching the stars shining like tiny diamonds in space, and then this purple haze had descended.

Purple all around. It was bright and blinding. Peri screwed his eyelids tightly shut. He could hear Selene, Otto and Diesel stumbling around the Bridge.

'*S'fâh!*' Diesel shouted. 'What did you do, Otto?'

'I did nothing!' boomed Otto. 'Everything's just gone purple!'

Peri felt a change in the motion of the *Phoenix*. It speeded up, and shifted course.

'Something's taken control of us!' Selene shouted.

'How?' Peri asked. 'How could they get past our shields?'

Selene cleared her throat. 'That may be

my fault,' she said. 'I sent Boomerang messages on Ultrawave – to find out if anything's left of the Milky Way after the Xion attack. It's supposed to come back with replies attached. Something must be piggybacking on the return signal, using it to hack into our computer and control us.'

'Who would do that?' Diesel asked.

'Take your pick,' Peri said. 'The Xions and the Meigwors have both sworn to destroy us.'

'I don't think any Meigwor is smart enough to pull this off,' Diesel replied.

Peri heard a *swish* and *crack*, then a bellow of pain from Otto. He must have swung a punch at Diesel and hit the wall – in retaliation for the comment about his home planet.

'Missed!' Diesel jeered.

'We don't have time for fights,' Peri said.

'We need to take back control of the *Phoenix*.'

Peri had only recently discovered that he was part bionic with a special connection to the *Phoenix*. He would have to trust his instincts. Blindly, he beckoned to where he thought the control panel was hovering. He cheered when he felt it bump against his hands.

Then he felt a bigger bump at his back. Otto, Selene and Diesel were jostling him – and each other.

'Give me some room,' Selene said. Peri felt her hands grabbing for the control panel. 'I have to shut off the Ultrawave, so they can't pinpoint us any more.'

'Let's go Superluminal,' Diesel suggested, elbowing his way in.

Peri brushed Diesel's hands aside. 'It's not safe when we can't see.'

'Let's give it a shot anyway!' Otto boomed.

Peri felt the Meigwor's long, thick fingers fumbling over the control panel too. 'Which one's the Superluminal touchpad?'

'It's the red one,' Diesel said.

'But everything's purple!' Otto shouted.

'Exactly,' Peri said, holding the control panel close to his chest. 'Just back off, and let me and Selene figure this out.'

Otto and Diesel stepped back, muttering to themselves, one in Meigwor, the other in Martian.

Peri forced his eyes open. His eyeballs ached. He squinted through the purple fog at the control panel in his hands. All the controls were shades of purple. The ship was pulsing forward under someone else's command.

They hadn't come so far and escaped so many dangers just to be reeled in like a helpless fish. There had to be *something* he could do.

Chapter 2

Come on, Peri said to himself. *You can do it.*

He nudged Selene aside.

'Hey!' Selene said. 'What are you –'

Peri's hand touched a small lever at the bottom of the control panel. He didn't know what it did. But his bionic half seemed pretty sure it was the right one.

He pulled it.

The ship juddered with a horrible, shrieking, grinding noise.

Peri, Selene, Otto and Diesel were flung

back across the Bridge. They landed in a heap against the far wall.

'*Ch'açh!*' Diesel shouted. 'What did you do?'

'Look!' Peri said. He got to his feet. The purple mist was thinning. Soon there were only a few wisps of it left.

Through the 360-monitor, Peri saw the stars zooming away from them.

Away from them?

Suddenly, Peri realised what he'd done.

He laughed. 'I put us into reverse.'

'That was a genius idea,' Selene said as she got to her feet.

Peri felt a crackling in his cheeks. Bionic blushing. 'Oh, well – you know . . .'

'So the purple tracking beam overshot us?' Diesel asked.

'Yes – but I'd better cancel that Boom-erang message,' Selene said. 'Or they'll lock on to us again.' She pressed a few buttons, her hands a blur even to Peri.

The purple haze had completely disappeared. The *Phoenix* was getting back to normal. Not that Peri knew anything about normal any more. The ship's crew had been sucked through a vortex right into the middle of an intergalactic war, accidently kidnapped Prince Onix, rescued Selene from planet Meigwor and survived a crash landing on a moon-planet.

'The sooner we drop Prince Onix back on Xion, the sooner we can go home,' Peri said.

Otto had tricked Peri and Diesel. They thought they had rescued a Meigwor prince, not kidnapped a Xion one. Returning Prince Onix had turned out to be harder than they'd expected. He was sedated in the Med Centre now because he couldn't remember who he was.

'If there is a home to go back to,' Selene said. 'I never got a reply to my Boomerang messages. Xion blew up the IF Space Station. Maybe Earth's been destroyed too.'

'And Mars,' Diesel said.

'Maybe the whole solar system — the whole galaxy is gone,' Selene said.

'But we don't *know* that,' Peri said. He felt a hollow sensation in his belly, when he thought of Earth no longer existing. 'We have to hope.'

'It's worse for me than for you lot!' Otto said. 'I can never go home to Meigwor! I'd be arrested as soon as I touched down. And it's all thanks to you Milky Way monkeys!'

'Who are you calling a monkey, you massive . . . lumpy-necked . . .' Diesel was so angry, he couldn't even finish his insult.

Peri heard a sound like two Jovian nose

flutes playing a duet. Three lights were winking on the control panel.

'That's the Ultrawave responding,' Selene said. 'We've got messages. They could be from the Milky Way.'

She reached for the control panel. Peri grabbed her wrist.

'Wait!' he said. 'It might not be the Milky Way — it could be our enemies, trying to trick us . . . Better scramble our signal, so they can't pinpoint us again.'

'Good thinking,' Selene said. 'I'll use the Twister. Kind of old school, but it works.' She pulled two long rubbery strings, like Martian sandworms, from a cavity next to the screen and knotted them together. 'Now if they try to get a fix on us they'll only get each other's coordinates.'

She touched each of the winking lights.

One whole side of the 360-monitor

filled up with the face of a Xion in full battle gear. Two spikes protruded from the mouth area of the black helmet, like insect jaws. A crown of some dull grey metal sat on top of the helmet, two antennae springing out from it. It was the king of Xion.

The other 180 degrees of the monitor were taken up with the huge head of Meigwor General Rouwgim. His thick, wrinkled crimson neck was curved like a letter S. His beady black eyes gleamed with anger.

'Not messages from the Milky Way, then,' Peri muttered.

The two giant heads began shouting at the top of their voices. Peri struggled to separate what each one was saying.

'You evil space pirates —'

'— double-crossing devils —'

'— what have you done with —'

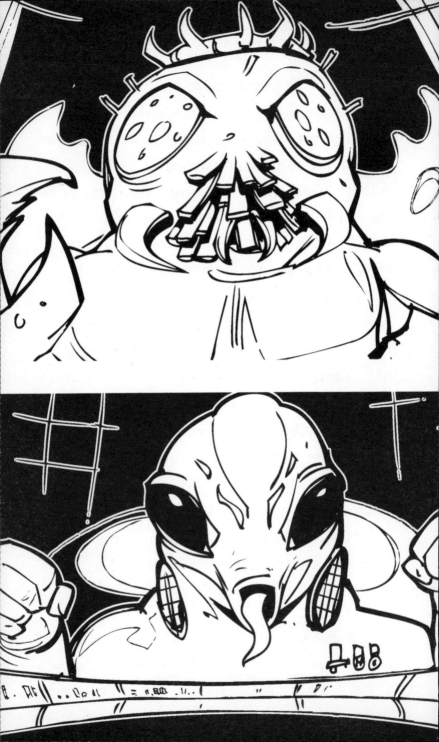

'— do you really think you —'

'— my son?'

'— can get away with this?'

'— if my son's been harmed —'

Peri faced the Xion king. 'Your son is fine. He was just — well, knocked out, that's all.'

'Who knocked him out?' roared the king. 'You will suffer for this!'

In the background, Peri heard Otto trying to calm General Rouwgim. 'I didn't mean it to turn out like this —'

'Last time, I saw you, Otto,' said General Rouwgim, 'you insulted me! You told me to stick my head under my armpit and take a deep breath!'

'No, that was a lie. I was imprisoned —'

'You, a Meigwor bounty hunter, imprisoned by those inferior life forms? I don't believe it!'

On the other side of the Bridge, the Xion king leaned in close, his nose and eyes nearly filling his half of the screen. 'Who's that?' he said. 'Is it that Meigwor pile of snake-dung, Rouwgim?'

'What?' Rouwgim boomed. 'Did I hear the squeaky voice of that crawling Xion king of the insects?'

'I'm going to obliterate you and all your kind!' the Xion king said.

'I'll squash you like a bug!' General Rouwgim shouted.

'Enough!' Diesel cried. He jumped forward and pulled out the two long rubbery strings, which created Selene's Twister. Instantly the voices stopped. The faces disappeared. The 360-monitor was once again blank.

'There's no point talking to them,' Diesel said. 'The Xions won't believe the prince is OK until we drop him on their doorstep. And the Meigwors will never listen to reason — they're just a bunch of dumboids. Let's dump the prince on Xion.' He jerked his thumb at Otto. 'We'll maroon this loser on an empty moon somewhere, then head back to the Milky Way and see what's left of it.'

Peri nodded. Diesel had spoken sense for once. 'I'll reset the course for Xion.'

'Wait a minute!' Otto said, very slowly, and very loudly. 'You lot wouldn't be alive without me!'

Peri noticed the black splotches around his mouth and eyes spreading over his face — a sure sign that Otto was getting angry. 'I can't go back to my own world, thanks to you — and now you want to maroon me?'

Otto shoved Diesel and Diesel shoved him right back. Otto's long tongue shot out and gripped Diesel by the arm. Diesel yelled in pain.

'Should we stop them?' Peri asked Selene.

'Let them get on with it,' Selene said. 'If we try to break it up we'll probably only get an elbow in the face.'

'Or Otto will give us a death bite,' Peri said. 'Or get us with his tongue.'

'Eee-ew!' Selene said.

The Bridge door slid open. Prince Onix came in, accompanied by a smell of Saturnian squid. He walked slowly, his eyes unfocused, as if he was sleepwalking. He was carrying a long red and white weapon.

'Look what I found,' he said. 'What is it?'

Peri looked at the weapon more closely. His heart did a somersault and a couple of cartwheels. It was an Orgmelter. He remembered it from weapons training at the IFA. *One of the deadliest weapons ever invented,* the instructor had said. *A one-second blast from this and your heart, liver, lungs and kidneys melt into porridge.*

'Just put it down, Prince Onix,' Peri said, backing away from the prince.

'Who's Prince Onix?' said Prince Onix.

'Where did he get it?' Peri whispered to Selene.

'Who cares?' Selene said. 'We just have to stop him using it.'

The prince fiddled with the controls on the side of the Orgmelter. It lit up, shining silver and crimson.

Diesel and Otto stopped fighting. Otto's neck craned round to stare at the prince. His eyes bulged as he saw the Orgmelter. 'No, you don't!' He lunged at Prince Onix, trying to swipe the weapon from his grasp.

Prince Onix pressed the trigger.

A laser beam fizzed just past Otto's head.

It hit one of the captain's chairs. The chair melted into a green puddle.

Otto held up his long, double-jointed arms in surrender.

Prince Onix inspected the Orgmelter curiously. Then he pointed it at Peri. 'I want to go home.'

Chapter 3

Prince Onix looked puzzled. He kept the Orgmelter pointing at Peri, although his finger came off the trigger. 'But how can I go home when I don't know where I come from?'

'You come from a planet called Xion,' Selene said. 'We'll take you there.'

Prince Onix turned to look at Selene. His eyes widened. His mouth dropped open, then curved into a foolish smile. 'Who are you?'

'I'm Selene, don't you remember?'

'If I'd met you before, I'm sure I'd remember,' the prince said.

'Yeah, right,' Selene said, shuddering. She clearly hated the prince's attention. 'Listen, will you do me a favour?'

'Anything for you, sweet Celery!'

Selene growled. 'It's Selene, not Celery,' she said. 'Give me that Orgmelter.'

As if in a trance, the prince handed over the weapon. Selene placed her free hand on the wall. 'Bits and bobs,' she said to the *Phoenix*. A drawer popped out. It held all kinds of useful things. Selene popped the Orgmelter into the bits and bobs drawer. 'Lock it,' she said and the drawer disappeared into the smooth wall of the Bridge. The prince grabbed her hand and bent low, as if to kiss it. Selene snatched her hand away.

Peri saw her take an adhesive patch out

of her pocket. The Sleepez! She'd already knocked the prince out once with it.

'No!' Peri said. 'If we're taking him home, you can't knock him out.'

Selene shrugged and put the Sleepez back in her pocket.

'You've already knocked me out,' the prince said adoringly.

Selene turned away and mimed being sick. Peri gave her a warning glare. He touched a button on the control panel and zoomed in on Xion. It was still a few million miles away, but it came up bright and clear, filling one side of the 360-monitor. The huge twisting orange ribbon of the space highway curled around it. In between its coils glistened the deadly blue Cos-Moat. Peri had hoped the sight might trigger memories for the prince. But he didn't even look at it. He only had eyes for Selene.

'Hey, Prince,' Peri said. 'Don't you want to see your home planet?'

The prince continued to gaze into Selene's eyes. 'Could I hold your hand?'

'Why don't you hold your own hand and pretend it's mine?' Selene said and tried to hide a smile.

Obediently, Prince Onix clasped his own hands together.

'I'm sick of this messing about,' Diesel

said. He grabbed the prince's arm and pulled him round so he was facing the monitor. 'That's your planet. How do we get on it without being stopped on the space highway or caught in the Cos-Moat and chewed up by space-sharks?'

The prince's eyes flitted over the screen for a couple of nanoseconds. 'Rubbish,' he said. Then he stared at Selene again.

'What?' Diesel's strip of hair was turning red and sticking up like the bristles of an angry porcupine. 'How dare you —'

Selene stepped in between the prince and Diesel. 'Don't you see? He's solved the problem.'

Peri looked at her, baffled.

She went over to the control panel. The prince trotted behind her like a puppy at her heels. She twiddled a dial on the monitor controls. She'd switched it to infrared vision — that meant the monitor picked up heat traces. In this new view, the space highway and the Cos-Moat were hardly visible, because they gave off little heat. But a giant red column could be seen clearly, spewing out flame, smoke and ashes from the planet.

'Xion incinerates all its rubbish and blows it out into space,' Selene said.

'What's so great about that?' Otto said. 'We do it on Meigwor; everybody does it.'

'They did it on Earth, way back,' Selene said. 'Until they banned it with the Clean Space Act of 2098. It had got so polluted they could hardly see the Moon.'

'Get to the point,' Diesel said impatiently.

'Instead of going down the rubbish chute, we go up it,' Selene said. 'Top marks to Onix.'

The prince grinned at her. 'I live to serve you.'

'I think that sonic dart must have frazzled his brain,' Diesel muttered. 'And, if we try and go up the chute, we'll be burnt to a crisp,' Diesel said.

Peri watched a column of flame erupt. The fiery red glow faded. 'See how it comes and goes?' he said. 'If we time it just right, we can zoom to the planet in between the bursts.'

'If it's like the one on Meigwor, there'll be lots of smaller chutes joining into a giant one,' Otto said. 'One of the chutes will lead directly to the incinerator. We don't want to go down that!'

Peri studied the column of flames as they powered up again. 'Twenty-three seconds, sixteen micro-seconds and five nanoseconds between blasts,' he said. Somehow, his bionic brain knew the exact time. 'I hope that will be long enough.'

They set a direct course and were soon hovering a few hundred miles above Xion. Peri wiped the sweat from his forehead. The Bridge had grown hot. Even with the *Phoenix*'s thermo-dials turned all the way to 'Arctic', the heat from the Xion rubbish incinerator was stifling. Diesel was gasping for breath.

'I reckon we're close enough,' Peri said. 'Time to start the descent.'

'OK – you take the Nav-wheel,' Selene said. 'I'll count us down. Diesel, can you man the Space Cannon? Blast any bits of debris that look like they're going to hit us.'

'Oh yeah!' Diesel took his place at the gunnery station.

'What am I going to do?' Otto said.

'And me!' the prince said. 'What about me?'

'You two just hold tight,' Peri said.

He turned the Nav-wheel until the column of flame, soot and ash was directly ahead. It licked out towards them hungrily – the tip of the flames only a few miles away.

'I'm counting down from five,' Selene said. 'At zero the flames will drop and we go. Five, four, three . . .'

Peri gripped the Nav-wheel.

'. . . two, one, zero!'

Peri pulled the booster levers.

The *Phoenix* dive-bombed.

The flames dropped away. Ahead, Peri saw the mouth of the metal chute, still glowing red.

It widened rapidly.

Darkness fell as they entered the chute.

Peri flicked on the outboard lights. The walls of the chute rushed by, curving one way and then the other. Desperately, Peri tried to keep the ship in the middle of the tunnel, without slowing down. Any miscalculation and they'd hit the side of the chute. At this speed, that would be the end of them.

Peri felt a tingling in his arms and legs. His bionic abilities were firing up. His reactions became super-fast. He threw the Nav-wheel from side to side as he followed the twists and turns of the chute.

'Fifteen seconds till incinerator powers up!' shouted Selene.

Peri saw chunks of rubbish explode and disintegrate into fragments as Diesel's missiles hit them.

'Nice shooting, Diesel!' he called.

'Ten seconds until it fires up!' Selene yelled.

Then Peri saw three black holes rushing towards them. It was a junction – the chute split three ways. He eased up on the boosters.

'What are you doing?' screamed Selene. 'Five seconds to go!'

'One of those must be the incinerator!' Otto said. 'Choose the wrong one and we're grilled.'

'Go left!' shouted Diesel.

'Go for the middle!' boomed Otto.

'Go right!' screamed Selene.

'What's happening?' said Prince Onix.

Peri made his choice.

Chapter 4

The *Phoenix* zoomed into the left-hand chute.

Peri heard a roar. A wave of red light lit up the Bridge.

But the light was behind them.

He'd guessed right.

'*Klûu'ah!*' Diesel said shakily. 'That was close.'

Prince Onix tried to hug Selene, but she dodged.

As the Bridge cooled, Peri's muscles relaxed. The tingling in his limbs stopped. He slowed the ship to a few hundred miles an hour. It would be silly to crash into anything now, after avoiding the incinerator.

The chute widened. And straightened. The outboard lights lit up what looked like a mountain. A mountain of sludgy brown and muddy red and sickly green and radioactive blue. Peri reached for the boosters, to try slowing the *Phoenix*, but he reacted too late – they hit the mountain with a soft thump, the ship burying itself in the mountain.

A mountain of rubbish.

The 360-monitor showed slimy, decaying food, old bandages and various bits of rusting Xion mining machinery. There were also bits of broken-up battlecruisers, and other piles of bubbling slime.

'We need to get moving. We'll have to go through this mess,' Selene said.

'Why can't we fly in like we did before?' Diesel asked.

'Xion's defence systems will be on red alert this time,' Peri explained. 'If we take the ship in closer to the palace, we're bound to be spotted.'

He tapped the nano-button implanted in his ribs, coughed and felt his lungs expand. The hydro-bubble had kicked in; now he'd be able to breathe freely in Xion's carbon-rich atmosphere. Selene and Diesel did the same. Robot arms shot out from the wall and replaced the thick magnetic soles of their space boots with thinner soles, suitable for Xion gravity.

'Prince – do you know the way to the palace from here?'

'What palace?' the prince asked.

Selene rolled her eyes. 'Better use the Quikmap.'

Peri engaged the Quikmap 7000 touch-pad on the control panel. 'Palace of the Xion royal family, please.'

A purple ball shot from the ship. Peri saw it whizz over the mountain of garbage and disappear. A moment later, it beamed back images to the Quikmap 7000 monitor screen. There was a wide, grassy plain. It looked like Earth grass, except that it was red. The orb raced across it. Then there were miles of coalfields with tall chimneys, mining machinery and clouds of black smoke.

Then, at last, a town.

On a hill in the middle of the town was a palace with tall, spiky white towers, slightly stained with soot. The Quikmap orb came to a stop. The words RANGE: 102 MILES came up on the monitor.

'Could be worse,' Peri said.

They left the Bridge and went down the mauve-lit corridor. Peri touched the exit panel. The wall slid open and a ramp appeared, leading into the heart of the rubbish.

The smell hit Peri as soon as he set foot on the ramp. He gagged. The Expedition Wear helmet smoothly rose and covered his head. It shut out some of the smell. But not all of it.

Diesel took two wads of Eterni-chew gum from his pockets. He stuffed one in his mouth, and pushed the other up his nostrils. 'That's better,' he said.

'We need to cloak the ship,' Selene said.

'Cloaking won't be enough,' Peri said. 'That won't stop it from getting shovelled into the incinerator.'

He looked at the control strip on the wristband of his Expedition Wear. He wasn't sure what to do. But his bionic half was gradually learning more and more about the *Phoenix*'s powers. It made the decision for him. One of the dials was labelled Expansion Packs. Peri twisted the dial anticlockwise.

The *Phoenix* shrank.

And shrank.

And shrank.

At last it was the size of a toy.

'Wow!' Selene said.

Peri picked up the *Phoenix* and slipped it in his pocket. 'OK, let's get moving.'

They climbed up the rubbish heap. It felt horribly soft and slimy underfoot. They got to the top and saw more rubbish mountains. Miles and miles of them, as far as the eye could see.

'I don't like this place,' the prince said.

'But this is your home planet,' Selene replied.

'It can't be,' the prince said. 'I'm sure my home planet is a beautiful place. But this is revolti— *Eeeek!*'

The prince gave a sudden squeal and leapt into Selene's arms. She staggered and dropped him. 'What are you doing?' she said crossly.

'There are horrible creatures!' Prince Onix said, dancing on the tips of his toes. He pointed with a shaking finger.

Peri saw twitching snouts poking through the stinking mounds of rubbish.

Rats! They were not quite like Earth rats. They had scaly, yellow, hairless skin. They had extra mouths at the side of their heads, just below the ears. They opened their mouths and squeaked horribly, each showing three sets of needle-sharp teeth.

Then they came swarming over the rubbish towards the *Phoenix*'s crew.

Peri snatched the laser from the belt of his Expedition Wear and shot the rat closest to him. It rolled over and lay still. Two other rats instantly jumped on it and started nibbling.

'*Urgh!*' squealed Otto. 'Rats! Help!'

'You're scared of rats?' jeered Diesel. 'Some bounty hunter you are! *Ch'ach!*' He jumped back just in time to avoid the rat snapping at his leg.

Selene shot it. But more and more rats were appearing from the deepest, darkest cracks in the rubbish. The crew were surrounded by them.

'Mummy!' shrieked Otto.

'Help!' Prince Onix whined. The rats crept closer, squeaking. Saliva dripped from their needle teeth.

'We have to get out of here,' Selene said. 'We can't fight them off, there are too many!'

'Press the Zero-G button on your ankle!'
Peri called to his crew.

He pressed his and immediately rose into
the air. Selene and Diesel joined him a
moment later.

Otto and the prince were still on the
ground. Otto was flapping his arms wildly,
shrieking.

Selene grabbed Onix under the armpits
and lifted him clear.

It took both Peri and Diesel to lift Otto. With his free hand, Peri fired his laser again. He hit two rats, which were gobbled up by the five more that emerged from the rubbish.

The Zero-G carried the *Phoenix* crew on over the rubbish heaps, just above the snapping jaws of the leaping rats. Otto thrashed around so much that Peri and Diesel kept dropping him. They ended up carrying him by his feet.

At last, they left the rubbish heaps behind. The squeak of the rats died away.

'That was the worst thing that's ever happened to me!' moaned Otto.

'Let's dump the prince and split,' Diesel said. 'This planet isn't any too friendly. We've brought him back home. Isn't that enough?'

'He'd never find his way to the royal

palace alone,' Peri said. 'And if anything else happens to him, it's us they'll blame.'

'Peri's right,' Selene said. 'We have to take him all the way. It's only about a hundred miles.'

'*Only!?*' groaned Diesel and Otto at the same time.

After a while they got the hang of zooming along in Zero-G. Selene carried the prince. Peri and Diesel carried Otto. The red, grassy plain scooted by beneath them. Then the black mining country, that seemed to go on for ever. Later in the day, they finally reached the dark, sooty buildings and narrow streets of Xion's capital city.

'Better walk from here,' Peri said. 'We'd be pretty easy to spot flying along.'

They touched their Zero-G buttons and dropped to the ground with a gentle bump.

Otto wound his arms round his back and pulled up his cape collar to conceal his neck. A few people stared at them as they walked through the streets. Luckily, they didn't need to ask for directions — the marble towers of the palace were easy to spot.

They were only a few streets away when a group of Xion guards appeared in the road ahead. They were dressed in battle gear, with black chest armour, antennae sprouting from their helmets and pincer-like gloves. They carried laserpulses. At the sight of the *Phoenix*'s crew in their Expedition Wear, they quickened their pace.

'Halt!' shouted the leader.

Peri, Selene, Diesel and Otto looked at each other in dismay.

'What do we do?' Diesel said.

'I think,' Peri said, 'that we should run!'

Chapter 5

Peri led the way, looking for somewhere to hide. He bolted round a street corner. There was a low green door set into a wall. Peri yanked it open and they all piled through.

They found themselves in a tavern. It reminded Peri of saloon bars he'd seen in old movies from planet Earth, called 'westerns'. People of all species were sitting at wooden tables drinking foaming green ale from which clouds of smoke arose. As well as the Xion customers, Peri recognised

Saturnians, Betelgeusians, Sirians, and a group of Alpha Centaurians who had humanoid heads and horse-like bodies. They were all talking and shouting and laughing.

At the sight of Peri and the crew, they fell silent. The ten-tentacled Aldebaranian who had been playing the piano stopped playing.

Every head turned to stare at them.

'Er – hi,' Peri said awkwardly.

The silence continued. Then the customers shrugged and turned back to their drinking, and the noise level rose again.

'They're used to seeing strangers here,' said Otto. 'It's a mining planet – people come here from all over the galaxy to find work.'

'What now?' Diesel said.

'Let's just hide out here,' Peri said. He led

the group to an empty table in a dark corner, taking care to keep between Prince Onix and the people at the bar. 'We'll look and see if the coast is clear in a while.'

A Xion waiter came and stood by their table. 'To drink?'

'Just water,' Peri said.

The waiter raised his eyebrows. 'You have expensive tastes, my friend.'

'Expensive?'

'Water is the most expensive drink on Xion. That will be sixty-one thousand creds, please.'

The door of the tavern was kicked open. The Xion guards marched in. Their antennae quivered as they scanned the room.

'We're looking for some strangers,' the leader barked.

Uh-oh, Peri thought. *Trouble.* The others

were looking at him anxiously. 'Has anyone seen any aliens?' demanded the leader of the guards.

'We're all aliens here,' said an Arcturusian, with eyes the size of plates and a wrinkled pink trunk.

The guard continued, 'I mean aliens who've just come in –'

Peri's mind went Superluminal. He had to create a distraction. That was the only hope they had of slipping away unnoticed. And what better distraction than a fight.

'– you Arcturusian monstrosity!' Peri yelled, mimicking the guard's barking voice.

'What did you call me?' The Arcturusian took a step towards the guard.

'– you Xion heap of space-shark droppings?' added Peri, in a perfect imitation of the Arcturusian's nasal tones.

The leader of the guards rushed at the Arcturusian with his arm upraised. The Arcturusian's trunk shot out and whacked the guard on the nose. Another guard ran up and pushed the Arcturusian, who fell over a table, breaking it.

'Get down,' Peri told his crew.

A bottle crashed on the wall above Selene's head. They all ducked behind the table.

The Arcturusian's friend, one of the Alpha Centaurians, kicked out with his hooves and sent the guard flying. Another guard whacked the Alpha Centaurian with his laserpulse. Then someone broke a chair over that guard's head. Soon the whole tavern had joined in the fight and furniture and glasses and fists were flying everywhere.

'Let's get out of here,' Peri said.

'But I love a good fight!' Otto said. He

unfolded his arms and rushed forward.

'There's no time for fighting, Otto!' Peri said, grabbing Otto by one arm. Diesel grabbed Otto by the other arm, and Selene pushed him from behind. Together, they propelled him through the door. Prince Onix followed, sticking close to Selene.

'This way,' Peri said. They set off at a run towards the palace. Soon it was looming right over them.

'That's your home, Prince,' Selene said. 'Recognise it?'

The prince shook his head. 'Never seen it before in my life.'

'Well, that's where you're going,' Peri said, as they walked towards the palace gates. They passed through an archway made from the twisted wreckage of spaceships destroyed in battle. Peri drew the prince into the archway's shadow. 'I'm giving you a message to take to your mum and dad, OK?' he said.

He pulled the Holographiser from the breast pocket of his Expedition Wear. This was a flexible, mirrored pad, into which the sender spoke. The message was then delivered as a 3-D holograph when the recipient opened it.

'Dear King and Queen — we are returning Prince Onix safe and sound. He was taken by mistake. He seems to have lost his memory but he'll soon get that back. Probably. Apologies and best wishes, Peri, of Planet Earth. If it still exists.'

Peri folded the Holographiser and stuck the adhesive side to the prince's tunic. 'All right? Off you go.' He pointed to the whitish towers of the royal palace. 'Just knock on the door – they'll be so glad to see you!' Peri said.

'But will I be glad to see them?' Prince Onix asked.

'Of course you will!' Selene said. 'They're your mum and dad.'

'I'd rather stay with you,' the prince said. 'With Selene.'

'Look, Prince,' Peri said. 'Just go home!'

'Go home!' Selene said.

'Go home!' Diesel said.

'Go home!' Otto said.

'Well, since you put it like that . . .' the prince said. He stood thinking for a while. Then he pulled off the Holographiser, crumpled it up, and dropped it to the ground. 'I've decided I feel most at home with you. We'll travel all over the universe together in the *Phoenix!*'

'No, we won't,' Selene said, turning the

prince towards the palace and giving him a gentle push forward.

There was a shout. The Xion guards from the tavern were running up the street towards them. They were battered and bruised and their clothing was torn. And they were angry.

Very angry.

'Get them!' shouted the leader.

'Let's fight!' Diesel said.

Otto turned to Diesel, flexing his arms. 'I thought you'd never ask.'

'Not each other, you voidoid!' Peri shouted. 'Them!'

The guards surrounded them. Diesel dropped into the classic cosmic-combat position. So did Otto. His tongue flickered in and out menacingly.

The leader of the guard produced a thick shiny cylinder from a holster on his belt.

He took aim and fired. A blue flash lit up
Diesel and Otto.

And then they were frozen into statues.

Chapter 6

Diesel and Otto toppled to the ground. They didn't move. Diesel's legs were still bent and his fists still clenched. Otto's tongue was still sticking out of his mouth.

The leader of the guard aimed his weapon at Peri.

'Wait!' Peri cried. 'We come in peace. Look – we've brought your prince back!'

'A likely story,' said their leader. Then he looked more closely. 'Bubbling sludge! It *is* the prince!' He spoke into a com-clip attached to his helmet. 'This is Captain

Grinkox at Archway One. We have Prince Onix here. Repeat: we have Prince Onix at Archway One.'

Peri grabbed Selene's arm and started to back away.

'You're going nowhere!' said Captain Grinkox.

Peri reached into his pocket. If he grew the *Phoenix* to full size now, he and his friends might be able to use the surprise and confusion to escape.

Captain Grinkox saw the movement. He blasted Peri with his strange weapon. Peri felt as if he'd been covered in a cloud of freezing blue gas. He couldn't move a muscle.

The captain blasted Selene too. She froze and keeled over, her arms and legs sticking out at odd angles.

'Search them!' the captain said to his men.

One of the guards pulled the *Phoenix* from Peri's pocket. 'Found this toy egg, Captain.'

'That's a funny little thing,' said Captain Grinkox, inspecting it. 'I'll give it to my little boy to play with.' He tucked the *Phoenix* under his helmet.

Peri wanted to shout that it wasn't a toy, it wouldn't be safe to play with, and anyway it wasn't the captain's to give to anyone.

But he couldn't utter a sound.

The guards loaded Peri, Selene, Diesel and Otto into hoverbarrows. Dumped on his back, Peri could see nothing but sky, and the bobbing antennae of Captain Grinkox's helmet.

'What have you done to my friends?' he heard the prince say.

'They're not your friends, Your Highness.'

The guards began to push the hover-barrows towards the palace. Peri watched the orange sky pass by above. A jolt sent Otto tumbling against him, so that his tongue touched Peri's ear. Peri strained to move away, but couldn't.

There was a fanfare of Xion trumpets, which sounded like someone sitting on a set of old Earth bagpipes.

'Your Majesties!' Peri heard Captain Grinkox say. 'Your son is here – and I have arrested his kidnappers.'

Peri was just able to see the royal couple as they stepped closer. They were humanoid, except for the webbed hands and the squid-like smell. They had sharp, pointed noses and teeth. The king wore a crown of some dull grey metal with huge spikes sticking up out of it; the queen wore a similar one in white.

'Oh, my precious Onix!' said the queen.

'Welcome home, son!' said the king.

'Who are you?' the prince asked.

The queen moved out of sight. Peri heard a scuffling sound, as if she was trying to hug Onix and he was pulling away. 'Don't you remember me?' she asked pleadingly.

'Should I?'

'We'll get your memory back, my boy,' the king said. 'Top doctors will work on it. And never fear – your abductors will be

punished. We will show them no mercy! Captain – take them to the dungeons!'

'Can I go with them?' asked the prince.

'Don't be silly,' said the queen. 'You are coming home with us!'

'I don't want to go with you,' the prince said sulkily. 'I want to go with my friends.'

The king came and stood over Peri. 'We Xions are a fair people. You will have a fair trial. And after the fair trial, you Meigwor-lovers will wish you had never been born!'

The guards tipped Peri and his frozen crew down the palace steps and let them bump to the bottom. The palace dungeons were dark. And damp. And dreary.

Two guards followed them down and clamped Otto's wrists in a pair of massive steel cuffs. The cuffs were then chained to the wall, so that Otto had to stand with his arms above his head. They covered Otto's neck-bumps with stick-on patches, so he wouldn't be able to use the hypnotic powers Peri and Diesel had seen him use when they kidnapped the prince.

'Stay there, Meigwor scum!' said one of the guards. 'The rest of you, keep quiet or you'll be chained up too.'

He left, banging the huge metal-studded door behind him. Peri heard the key turn in the lock.

The effect of the Xion weapon was beginning to wear off. Peri rubbed his arms and legs, which had pins and needles. He looked round. There was a tiny barred window, high up. A few feeble rays of light sneaked in. Apart from that, nothing but stone walls.

Dark shapes moved across the floor. One scuttled over Otto's feet. He shrieked. 'Was that a rat?'

'No,' Selene said. 'Just a giant cockroach.'

'You'd better enjoy these delightful surroundings while you can,' said a quiet voice.

Peri spun round and saw a figure sitting hunched in the corner. It had a grey, cement-like body, but no head. It was holding up its hands, palms outwards. In the centre of each palm was a single, staring eye. A Zaxonian. From Zaxos. Peri had never met one before, but had learned about them at the IFA in the intelligent life-forms module. They had mouths where you'd expect their belly-buttons to be. He looked – sure enough, there was a mouth set into its middle. 'What are you in for?' the Zaxonian said, turning its hands over. On the back of each hand was an ear.

'Kidnapping the prince,' Peri said. 'But we didn't do it.'

'I'm in for being a space highwayman,' said the Zaxonian. 'And I did do that.'

'Cool!' Diesel said. 'You robbed space-ships, yeah?'

'That's right. On my last raid I robbed a banking ship and got away with fifty-seven million creds and a hat — which I couldn't wear, obviously, but it was a really nice one.' The Zaxonian sighed. 'I'm Tambo, by the way.'

'So what's going to happen to you now?' asked Selene.

'Same thing that will happen to you. A big live public trial. It's their favourite entertainment. First they watch the trial, then the punishment.'

'What if the accused gets off?' asked Peri.

Tambo opened his belly-mouth to answer but, before he could, a hole in the floor suddenly opened beneath him. He slid down a chute, screaming the whole way. Peri thought he could hear distant cheering. The trapdoor snapped shut. All was quiet again.

'We have to get out of here!' Diesel said. He examined the brickwork, searching for gaps with his fingernails.

'What about me?' Otto said, rattling his chains.

'You deserve the trial,' Diesel said. 'This is all your fault!'

'We can't leave him!' Peri said. Otto was not exactly his favourite alien, but they were in this together. 'We're a team. We have to free Otto and take him with us. Don't you agree, Selene?'

'Er – yeah, I suppose,' Selene said uncertainly.

'I'll call the *Phoenix*!' Peri said. 'That'll get us out of here.'

He closed his eyes and tuned into his bionic half. He sent out a telepathic message: *Phoenix. We need you. Come here now!*

Nothing happened.

'Maybe the guard's helmet is blocking the signal,' Selene said.

Peri felt sick with disappointment. But he didn't give up.

'Let's try the door,' he said. He ran up the steps. Before he got to the door, he hit an invisible force field which almost knocked him back down the steps.

'Let's try the window!' Selene said.

Peri ran back down. He and Diesel hoisted Selene up so she could reach for the bars, but another invisible force field pushed her backwards. All three of them tumbled to the floor.

Peri rose to his feet. He seized Otto's chain, trying to wrench it from the wall. It gave him an electric shock which zapped him right across the dungeon.

He braced himself to hit the floor hard. But he didn't.

Because the floor had opened up again . . .

Chapter 7

Peri went whirling down a curly slide in total darkness. He landed with a bump on a sandy surface. Selene, Diesel and Otto tumbled on to the ground next to him.

A spotlight hit them. Peri saw the other three, looking as bewildered as he felt. Beyond the circle of light it was pitch-black. He heard the buzz and murmur of a crowd. It grew louder as a man stepped into the spotlight.

The man was dressed in a black gown and wore a white wig. He looked to Peri like the old-time planet Earth lawyers that he had seen in time-travel simulators in his history lessons at the IFA. But the webbed hands and squid-like smell revealed him as a Xion.

'I am your lawyer,' he said.

'Great!' Selene said. 'So you're going to try to get us off?'

There was a burst of laughter from the unseen crowd.

'Excuse me,' Peri said. 'But why are you in that costume? That's how lawyers on Earth used to dress –'

'They copied it from us!' the lawyer said. 'Lawyers have dressed like this for at least a hundred years on Xion.'

'But they used to dress like that on Earth thousands of years ago!'

The lawyer looked sternly down his pointed nose at Peri. 'As I said, Xion lawyers have dressed like this for many thousands of years. Everyone knows that Earthlings are the biggest copycats in the universe!'

There was a roar of approval from the crowd.

'Now,' the lawyer said, 'if you plead guilty to the charges, I can possibly get your sentence reduced to twenty-five years in the sludge mines.'

'What are the charges?' Diesel asked.

'That,' said the lawyer, 'is none of your business.'

'But how can we plead guilty if we don't know the charges?' Peri protested.

'You're being difficult – very difficult!' said the lawyer. The crowd hissed and booed. 'Do you plead guilty or not?'

Peri looked at the others. Selene shrugged. Diesel pointed at Otto. 'He's guilty!'

Otto glared at him.

'We all plead not guilty!' Peri said. It wouldn't help to try to make Otto take the rap. Anyway, it wouldn't be fair – it wasn't Otto's fault that the prince had lost his memory. They were all in this together now.

The lawyer smiled, exposing two rows of shark-like teeth. 'Then let the trial begin!'

Suddenly the whole area was drenched in bright light. Peri gasped. They were in the middle of a vast arena. There were banks of tiered seating all around, filled with thousands of Xion spectators. Flags fluttered from tall poles. Above the highest seats were giant monitors, which showed Peri and his friends from every angle, standing small and isolated – and surrounded.

The king and queen of Xion sat in the best seats, in a raised box in the front row, decorated with Bio-Cloth, which swirled with constantly changing living colours. Prince Onix, looking completely confused, sat between his mother and father. He caught Selene's eye and waved. His father pulled his arm down.

In front of the royal box, at ground level, were three judges, sitting behind a bench. They all wore black robes, and had even longer wigs than the lawyer.

The lawyer sat on a chair to one side of the judges. 'Take it away, boys,' he said.

A judge jumped to his feet. He came out from behind the bench and paced up and down in front of the accused. He pointed a webbed finger at them. 'What made you decide to become sworn enemies of Xion?'

'Nothing,' Selene said, 'because —'

The crowd booed. They threw tiny pebbles. One hit Peri on the back of the neck.

'"*Nothing?*"' screeched the judge. 'You became sworn enemies of Xion for no reason?'

'Wait!' Peri shouted above the crowd's roar. 'This isn't fair!' He appealed to their lawyer. 'Aren't you going to defend us?'

'Why should I?' said the lawyer. 'You said you weren't guilty, so you must be liars. I don't defend liars.'

The crowd roared. They threw more pebbles. They had it in for Otto particularly. He covered his head with his double-jointed arms.

The first judge sat down and the next jumped up. 'When did you Earthlings start obeying the orders of the evil Meigwors?'

'We didn't!' Diesel said indignantly. He started towards the judges' bench. Peri grabbed his arm and pulled him back.

The second judge sneered. 'So the kidnap

of our beloved prince, and the deliberate erasing of his memory, was your own idea?'

'That's not what I said!'

'Yes it is!' screamed the first judge.

The crowd's roar rose to a frightening level. They threw more pebbles.

The third judge jumped up. He had a bigger wig than the others.

Maybe he's the chief judge, Peri thought.

'Call the first witness!' the judge shouted.

The first witness was Prince Onix. He stood up in the royal box.

'Now,' said the chief judge, 'tell the court, in your own words, about the terrible mistreatment you suffered aboard the spaceship of these evil criminals.'

'I don't remember much . . .' the prince began.

'Because they wiped your memory!' said the judge.

The crowd hissed. A storm of pebbles rained down on the crew of the *Phoenix*.

'But I do remember they were nice to me,' went on the prince. 'Especially Selene.' He pointed at her. 'But they're all my friends.'

The crowd hushed, then started to mutter uncertainly. The judges looked angry. Peri felt a twinge of hope.

The lawyer jumped up. 'The prince has just given cast-iron evidence that they brainwashed him!'

'Hey!' Peri said. 'You're supposed to be on our side.'

'I'm on the side of justice,' said the lawyer, with a wave to the spectators. The crowd cheered.

'The witness may stand down,' the first judge said. 'Next witness – the evil Meigwor! Approach!'

Otto approached the bench, flinching as if expecting more stones to rain down on him any moment.

The second judge pointed at him. 'Question for the evil Meigwor! Why do you hate Xion so much?'

There was a sudden hush. Otto licked his lipless mouth nervously with his supersize tongue. 'I don't exactly hate Xion –' he began.

A pebble whizzed through the air and bounced off his head.

'Ow! If the Xion coward who threw that comes down here, I'll push his pointy teeth down his throat!'

The spectators gasped.

'I've just remembered something!' Prince Onix called out. 'It was him – he was the one who kidnapped me.'

A hail of pebbles descended on Otto.

'No further proof is needed of this prisoner's hatred for Xion!' screamed the chief judge.

'Hold on!' Peri said, fighting to make himself heard above the roar. 'If we'd meant any harm to the prince, we wouldn't have brought him back –'

'Silence!' shouted the chief judge. 'No more of your lies. Time for the vote!' He surveyed the spectators. The other two judges stood up beside him. 'Ladies and gentlemen of Xion. You have heard evidence which proves that these criminals are guilty of kidnapping our beloved prince. He cannot even remember his own people now. Please touch the panel in front of you to deliver your verdict. Remember: green means they've got away with it, and red means they are *guilty*.'

Peri looked hopelessly at the other crew members. They looked hopelessly back.

The whole arena was lit up in a blaze of red.

Except, in the middle of the sea of red, Peri saw one solitary green light.

It was kind of comforting that one person in Xion didn't believe them to be guilty.

Not that it did them much good.

Chapter 8

'Miserable wretches — choose your punishment!' the chief judge said. 'You may toil in the sludge mines for fifty years. Or you may fight to the death with . . . the Xio-Bot!'

There were *oohs* and *aahs* from the crowd.

'You may confer!' the judge said.

Peri and the other crew members formed a huddle in the centre of the arena.

'What are we going to do?' Peri asked. He couldn't believe this was happening.

'If we go down the sludge mines, at least we stay alive,' Selene paused and lowered her voice. 'And have a better chance of escaping.'

'I say we face the Xio-Bot!' Diesel said. 'We have a fighting chance of winning and getting off this horrible planet straight away.'

Otto spoke through gritted teeth. 'I . . . I . . . I agree with Diesel!'

'But we don't even know what the Xio-Bot is!' Selene said.

'We don't know what the sludge mines are, either,' Peri said. He turned to the lawyer. 'What's it like down the sludge mines?'

Their lawyer smiled. 'Hell.'

'So you'd choose the Xio-Bot?'

'That would make you more popular with the crowd,' the lawyer said.

'Come on!' Diesel said. 'It's our only chance!'

'Yeah!' Otto said. 'Let's do it!'

'Ladies and gentlemen, the evil aliens

have chosen to fight the Xio-Bot!' said the chief judge. 'Give them a round of applause for being such good sports!'

There was cheering and laughter from the crowd. Hooters blared. Fireworks exploded in the sky.

'How many people have defeated the Xio-Bot?' Peri asked the lawyer.

'None,' the lawyer said, taking his seat.

A short, squat Xion man came pedalling into the arena on a golden tricycle. He wore a sparkly red jacket and a mirrored top hat. He must be the master of ceremonies.

'Ladies and gentlemen,' he bellowed, 'what a wonderful spectacle we have for you this afternoon. Four criminals versus the Xio-Bot! How long will they last?'

The noise of the crowd was deafening as everyone answered at once.

The Xion on the trike smiled. 'Place your bets on how long the criminals can stay alive in the ring with the terrifying Xio-Bot. We're offering one minute at evens, two minutes at odds of five to one. Or there's five minutes at a hundred to one. If you fancy a *really* long shot, we're offering odds of fifty-three billion, four hundred and ninety-two million, six hundred and seventeen thousand, six hundred and twenty-eight to one on them actually beating the Xio-Bot! You'll find official bookmakers to take bets in every row, easily recognisable by the windmills on their hats!'

There was a lot of toing and froing in the crowd as the spectators hurried to place bets.

'Without further ado, let's get on with the action!' said the master of ceremonies. He raised his hands above his head and clapped. The crowd joined in. The clapping grew louder and faster.

'We'll shut that crowd up!' growled Otto. 'We'll smash their precious Xio-Bot!'

'We need a plan to fight it,' Selene said.

'We should split up,' Diesel said. 'So it can't go for us all at once.'

'And when it goes for one of us,' Otto

said, 'the others attack from the sides and from behind.'

'Good plan,' Peri said. He held out his fist. Diesel, Selene and Otto did the same. They all bumped knuckles.

Two massive gates swung open. The crowd stopped clapping and roared instead. The master of ceremonies hastily pedalled to safety.

Peri felt his blood turn to iced water as a gigantic creature lumbered into the arena. It had to be six metres high. It looked something like a gigantic mutant grizzly bear from back home on planet Earth. It was covered in blue fur and had two robot arms and two robot legs. It had eyes on stalks which roved around, searching for prey. Two huge fangs, like giant walrus teeth, but made of metal, stuck out from its mouth.

The creature's eyes swivelled in their direction. It took a lumbering step.

'Split!' Diesel yelled.

Each of the crew ran to a different corner of the arena. The creature hesitated, then lumbered towards Otto. The crowd howled.

Diesel ran up behind it and tugged at its fur. It couldn't have hurt the beast, but it was enough to make it stop and turn. It lowered its massive head towards Diesel.

Peri picked up a handful of the pebbles that had been thrown and hurled them at the beast. One hit it in the eye, which retracted. The creature hissed. It lifted one of its huge metal feet. Peri dived to one side. The foot smashed down, making a massive dent in the ground where Peri had been standing just one second earlier.

The beast lifted its foot to try again. Peri saw the foot above him like a metal stamp about to descend. Selene caught his arm and pulled him clear.

At the same time, Otto sank his teeth into the Xio-Bot's flesh just above the monster's robotic leg. The Meigwor's powerful death-bite venom quickly began to take effect. Diesel ran to join him. They pushed together.

The creature was already off balance. It swayed, tottered and crashed face first to the ground. Peri heard the thud even above the noise of the crowd. Sand flew up. So did the creature's twin fangs, which had snapped off on impact.

But the beast was far from finished. It squealed with pain, and struggled to get to its feet, its robot legs kicking out wildly. Peri felt a pang of sympathy for it.

He snatched up one of the metal teeth and stood by its head. One of its eyes swivelled round and looked at him. It seemed to be pleading.

Peri stroked its fur. *Poor creature,* he thought. *A misfit, put together in a laboratory. Like me. Sent into the arena to fight without even knowing why.*

'Get on with it, Peri!' roared Otto.

'I – I don't think I can –'

The creature's robot arm rose up and swiped quickly at Peri. He ducked. Before it could strike again, he plunged the metal fang deep into its neck.

The creature gurgled. Its life blood ran out on to the sand.

The crowd went quiet.

'I'm sorry,' Peri whispered, wiping a tear from his eye. He turned to the judges. His voice was not quite steady as he said; 'Well – we fought and we won. Now you must keep your side of the bargain and let us go.'

The three judges stared back expression-lessly.

The crowd roared with laughter.

Hooters blared. Fireworks exploded. The master of ceremonies pedalled back in on his golden tricycle. 'Great warm-up, guys! Fantastic! And now it's time to face . . . the Xio-Bot!'

Chapter 9

'Is this really happening?' Peri said to Selene. 'Or are we in a nightmare?'

Selene was dusty and out of breath. Her face was scraped and bruised. 'I think it's real,' she said.

'Hey!' Diesel shouted to the judges. 'This isn't fair — we just beat the Xio-Bot!'

The master of ceremonies chuckled. 'That wasn't the Xio-Bot! That was the mini-Xio-Bot! Now, for the *real* Xio-Bot!'

Peri heard giant, crashing footsteps

approaching the arena, just before the massive gates flew open.

The Xio-Bot appeared.

Peri gazed in disbelief.

'How the *prrrip'chiq* are we supposed to defeat that?' Diesel said.

It made the fallen creature look tiny in comparison. The real Xio-Bot was twenty metres high. It was so big it didn't look like an animal. It was more like a moving, intelligent building.

Its roving eyes landed on the lifeless mini-bot.

The Xio-Bot let out a wail, the sound so furious and agonised that it made the hairs on the back of Peri's neck stand on end.

The Xio-Bot rushed into the arena with amazing speed for such a huge creature. Its metal arm extended and grabbed Otto.

The Meigwor howled as the Xio-Bot hurled him at the far wall.

Otto reacted fast. In midair he stretched out his double-jointed arm and grabbed a flagpole. He whizzed round it three times, then lost his grip and fell straight down into the royal box.

He crashed into Prince Onix, making one side of the royal box collapse. Otto and the prince fell sprawling on to the sand.

The Xio-Bot had already turned on the rest of the crew. It brought its giant metal foot crashing down on Diesel — or where Diesel would have been, if he hadn't dived out of the way. Selene got behind the beast, grabbed a handful of fur and began to climb up. Peri was impressed by her daring — but what was she trying to do? He didn't have time to wonder. The beast stooped and made a grab for him. He ducked beneath its clutching hand and flung himself to one side.

Out of the corner of his eye, he saw that Otto and the prince had got to their feet. They were looking at each other. The prince was holding his head, which had a bump from his fall.

'I remember!' the prince shouted. 'Stop the fight! These guys brought me home. They shouldn't have been put on trial.'

The crowd hushed. Everyone turned to stare at the prince. Peri felt a stab of hope.

'But they've been found guilty,' the king said. 'Justice must take its course.'

'Think how disappointed the spectators would be if we called off the fight now,' said the queen.

'But it's not fair!' shouted Prince Onix.

Distracted by watching this, Peri hadn't

noticed the Xio-Bot come up behind him until its metal hand closed around his middle. The pressure would have killed a normal human; but Peri's bionic inner shell held good.

For the moment.

The beast tightened its squeeze. Peri could hardly breathe. The Xio-Bot's eyes goggled at him. Any second now, and Peri knew he would crack.

But then the pressure eased. The beast's mouth dropped open. It gave a puzzled groan as Peri wriggled out of its grasp and dropped to the ground.

The Xio-Bot stood completely still.

Then it raised its arm. It extended a metal finger inside its ear. The finger emerged again, crooked around a brown, sticky, wriggling object.

With amazement, Peri recognised the object – Selene. She had climbed inside the beast's ear. She was covered in Xio-Bot earwax and held a twisted wire in her hand.

'Hey, it's all electrical circuitry inside there!' she yelled. 'If we could get in and –'

The beast held her at arm's length. From a height of fifteen metres, it dropped her.

Selene managed to grab the fur on its belly. This broke her fall momentarily, but she couldn't hang on.

Prince Onix sprinted forward from where he'd fallen from the royal box, throwing his body beneath Selene's, just as she landed, knocking him flat to the ground.

'Thanks,' Selene said.

'It's . . . my . . . pleasure . . .' gasped the prince, holding his ribs.

'Look out!' shouted Peri.

The Xio-Bot was charging towards them, squealing and roaring. It stamped straight past them, and kicked the arena wall. A benchful of spectators tumbled down into the arena. The Xio-Bot howled in triumph.

It's out of control, Peri realised. *Pulling that wire out of its ear has sent it completely crazy.*

'Stop the combat!' shouted the king. 'Enough!'

The master of ceremonies pedalled back into the arena. 'Er – Xio-Bot . . . Game over.' He pointed an oversized remote control at the beast and pressed the buttons frantically. Nothing happened.

The Xio-Bot put its foot against his tricycle and pushed, hard. The master of ceremonies whizzed across the sand and his trike smashed into pieces against the far wall.

'Send in the guards!' cried the king.

The Xio-Bot smashed another section of wall. A troop of guards, led by Captain Grinkox, ran in and fired their weapons at the Xio-Bot. But it was completely unaffected. It kicked out at the guards. They dodged, rolled and scattered.

'Guys!' called Peri. The *Phoenix* crew, and Prince Onix, ran towards him. 'That thing will destroy everyone unless we stop it! If me and Selene climb up and get inside, we can maybe short-circuit it. You and Otto distract it.'

'That's not fair!' Diesel said. 'Why do we have to be the bait in the trap?'

'I bet Otto's not afraid,' Peri said.

'Of course I'm not afraid!' boomed Otto.

'I'm not afraid either!' Diesel said angrily.

'Bring it on!' Prince Onix added, more quietly. He ran into the middle of the arena, clapping his hands. Otto and Diesel glanced at each other, then followed.

'Stupid old Xio-Bot!' shouted the prince. 'Bet you can't catch me!'

'Onix! Come away, it's too dangerous!' shouted his mother from the royal box.

The Xio-Bot's stalk-eyes settled on the prince, Otto and Diesel.

'Now!' Peri said to Selene. They grabbed the fur just above the creature's foot, and began to climb up its leg.

It was just like trying to climb a mountain – if that mountain could jump around.

The Xio-Bot was chasing the prince, Otto and Diesel around the arena, trying to squash them.

The guards were still blasting the beast, which had absolutely no effect.

Peri and Selene had almost reached the creature's massive head.

'Do we go in through the ear?' Peri asked Selene.

'No – it's too narrow, and you can't get in very far. The eye socket's a better bet.'

Peri didn't like the sound of that. But there was no choice. He grabbed a clump of fur on the Xio-Bot's neck and hauled himself up so that he was level with its face. Selene pulled herself up beside him. The Xio-Bot was still too busy trying to stamp on their friends to notice them.

'Ready?' Peri said. 'You take the left eye, I'll take the right!'

The Xio-Bot's eye-stalks emerged from metre-wide sockets. Peri squeezed his head in first, then his shoulders, then the rest of him inside. It felt cold and clammy, like the inside of an oyster. Darkness surrounded him as he clung on to a thick, gristly tendon. The creature's optic nerve, he guessed.

'Are you there, Selene?'

'Yes,' said a voice close by. 'But I can't see.'

'Hang on.' Peri flicked the illuminator switch on his helmet.

They were in a sort of cave, with wet red walls. The optic nerves he and Selene were holding on to were like thick cables leading down into a huge spongy mass. It looked a bit like a cauliflower, and smelt strongly of blue cheese.

'Look back along the optic nerve!' Selene said.

From their position, they could look

right through the creature's eyeballs. Peri saw their friends, looking tiny and vulnerable far below. They were running for their lives, keeping just ahead of the creature's crashing feet. They looked exhausted.

'What now?' Selene said.

There were no bits of trailing wire or circuitry in this part of the head. Peri thought about trying to attack the optic nerve – but it was too thick to break, and even a blinded Xio-Bot could still do a lot of damage. There was only one thing for it. He looked down at the giant spongy mass below.

'Wish me luck!' he said – and dived right into the brain.

Chapter 10

Peri hit the brain with a splat, and sank straight in. It was like falling into a giant, sloppy cauliflower cheese. He couldn't see anything. It was too dense for his illuminator to work. And he couldn't breathe. How long could he hold his breath — a minute, two minutes? Longer than that and he'd drown in the Xio-Bot's brain.

He floundered about in slow motion. He didn't know even what he was looking for. He was too small to cause enough damage to stop the beast just by swimming around in its huge brain. He had to do something to its circuitry – rewire it, or power it down somehow. But could he do that before his lungs burst?

Suddenly, Peri felt a tingling in his limbs. Strength surged through him. His bionic powers were kicking in!

He pushed his way down into the heart of the brain. His bionic nature intuitively understood the workings of this giant cyborg. His hands grasped a knot of wires that pulsed with energy. He pulled, but they didn't break. He was desperate to breathe; his chest felt as if it was on fire.

His hand followed the wires down. They ran into a metal box, hot to the touch. Peri ran his fingers along its sides. He located a plastic knob as thick and chunky as his own hand.

A lever? he thought. *Surely it can't be this easy?*

But his bionic half told him that it was. Using both hands, he tugged at the lever. There was a loud, juddering sound. The darkness was broken by sparks and flashes. Then the blackness returned, blacker than before, and with it, an eerie silence.

Peri felt the Xio-Bot lurch sideways. He got his feet on the metal box and pushed upwards, swimming as hard as he could through the gloopy mass. His head broke the surface. He sucked in lungfuls of air. He had never felt such relief in his life.

Selene was perched above him, shining her illuminator down. 'We have to get out,' she said. 'It's going to fall!'

The optic nerve she was sitting on swayed dangerously. She reached down. Peri grabbed her hand. She pulled. He jumped.

For a moment he hung on the optic nerve, legs scrabbling, in danger of slipping

back down into the brain. Then Selene hauled him up. They crawled up towards the eye socket, Selene first. Peri emerged after her, blinking in the light.

The Xio-Bot tottered like a struck skittle.

We have no time to climb back down, Peri realised. He saw one of the flagpoles, with its banner fluttering in the wind, about four metres away. Quite a leap – but it was their only chance.

'Jump, Selene!' he cried – and launched himself off the Xio-Bot's face.

His fingertips touched the flagpole and curled round it. *Yes!*

A moment later, he felt a violent tug on the leg of his Expedition Wear. Selene had missed the flagpole but caught him instead. They began to slide slowly down.

The Xio-Bot's legs buckled. It fell,

slowly at first and then faster as gravity took hold. It hit the ground so hard it bounced up again, before settling down, face first on the sand, a cloud of dust hovering around it.

Peri couldn't hold on any longer. Selene's weight was too much. He let go of the flagpole and they fell backwards.

Peri landed on the Xio-Bot's furry stomach. He bounced off like he had hit a trampoline, and landed feet first on the ground. Selene landed beside him.

The crowd cheered.

Diesel, the prince and even Otto ran up and high-fived them.

'Well done, Selene!' the prince said.

'That was *im-press-ive!*' Diesel said.

'You did pretty good,' Otto grunted, 'for Earthlings.'

Still the crowd cheered.

Then Peri heard another sound.

It sounded like . . . a siren.

A loud, blaring siren. Then a distant explosion.

The crowd began hurriedly evacuating, just as another explosion hit – this one close enough to make the arena shake.

The king and queen left the royal box. Two guards came and took Prince Onix by the hand and led him away. 'I'll see you

soon!' he said, looking back at Selene.

'Hurry, Your Highness!' said one of the guards. 'The Meigwors are attacking!'

'We have to get out of here!' Peri said.

Captain Grinkox and three guards strode towards them.

'Can I have my egg back?' Peri said. 'We can't leave without it.'

'You're not leaving,' said the captain, pointing a scary-looking weapon at him.

'But we've already beaten two generations of Xio-Bots,' Selene said.

'Yeah,' said Diesel. 'Who's next, the grandad?'

'Come with me,' said the captain and pointed his weapon at each of them in turn.

There was no choice but to obey.

They were taken by hovercar to a grim, fortress-like building.

The captain led them through a

corridor and down a steep, winding flight of steps. *Are we being taken to another dungeon?* Peri wondered.

Captain Grinkox unlocked a door, which slowly swung open. Peri noticed that the walls here were a metre thick. Inside the room sat the king and queen of Xion and Prince Onix.

'What's going on?' Peri said. 'Why are we under arrest?'

'You are not under arrest,' the king said. 'My son has told me of your prowess as Star Fighters. We would like your help in our fight against the Meigwors.'

Peri looked at Selene, Diesel and Otto. He considered his limited options. 'We'll help you,' he said. 'On two conditions. First, give us our spaceship back.'

'We do not have your spaceship,' the king said.

'He does,' Peri said, pointing at Captain Grinkox. 'You thought it was a toy egg. Come on, hand it over.'

Grinkox looked at the king. The king nodded impatiently. Grinkox took the *Phoenix* from his helmet and handed it over to Peri.

'Now for the second condition,' Peri said. 'If we help you, you have to stop all attacks against the Milky Way and send us back home.'

'Yes, yes, I promise!' said the king. 'As long as you help us defeat the Meigwors!'

Captain Grinkox cleared his throat. 'Your Majesty – what about this one?' He stared coldly at Otto. 'He *is* a Meigwor – we can't trust him.'

'Yes, you can!' Otto boomed. 'My own people have rejected me!'

'Let me go with them!' the prince said. 'I can help!'

'It wouldn't be safe, darling,' said the queen.

'Mum, I fought a Xio-Bot today,' Prince Onix whined.

The king nodded. 'It is Xion custom that a prince must earn his spurs in battle before he can succeed to the throne. I think your time has come, Onix.'

'*Yesss!*' the prince said, punching the air.

On the 360-monitor the dusty surface of planet Xion was fading behind them.

Peri and Selene sat side by side on the Bridge.

'You all right?' Selene said.

'Yeah, I'm — I'm fine,' Peri said, but all of his body was exhausted — human and robotic. It would be good to go back to Earth. *If Earth still exists,* he thought.

But there was no time for rest. Planet Earth was certainly doomed if they didn't beat their enemies.

'I'm fine,' he said again. 'Let's go sort out those Meigwors.'

A soft bleep from the control panel indicated that the ship's power cells were fully charged.

'Time to go Superluminal,' Peri said.

All they had to do now was defeat the Meigwors, save the Milky Way and somehow find their way home.

'Easy,' Peri whispered to himself, even though he knew it would be anything but.

Can Peri and the crew defeat
the Meigwors?

Will they ever make it back
to the Milky Way?

Find out! In . . .

Turn over to read Chapter 1

Chapter 1

'Follow that ship,' Prince Onix screamed across the Bridge of the *Phoenix*. He pointed at the Meigwor viper-ship snaking away from the dusty orange planet. 'Make them pay for attacking Xion!'

Peri pulled the thruster levers hard. The *Phoenix* raced after the enemy craft.

'Locking target trackers,' Diesel shouted. The half-Martian gunner cracked his knuckles. 'One X-plode detonator coming up.' He reached for the button on the gunnery station.

'Wait a nanosecond, Diesel,' Peri ordered. 'Why is that viper-ship leaving Xion? Where's the rest of the Meigwor fleet?'

'Who cares?' Diesel replied. 'You blast first and ask questions later.'

'Stop arguing and do something,' the prince snapped. 'You promised my father you'd destroy the Meigwors.'

Peri glared at him. 'We said we'd help save Xion as long as you never attack the Milky Way again. We need to find out what the Meigwors are up to — *then* we can start kicking some alien space-butts.'

'Watch out!' Diesel shouted as alarms erupted across the Bridge.

A huge purple and silver meteorite was plummeting towards them. Peri jerked the Nav-wheel sharply and slammed on the dodge mechanism. The *Phoenix* flew past it.

'What the *prrrip'chiq* was that?' Diesel asked.

'The s-s-space h-h-highway,' stammered Prince Onix. 'Look what the Meigwor have done.'

The twisty, twelve-hundred-lane space highway that had surrounded Xion had been shattered into gazillions of pieces. Huge chunks of Astrophalt were caught in orbit around the planet. The viper-ship started blasting its way through the debris.

Peri was not going to let it get away. He checked the *Phoenix*'s cloak and activated the sprint-thrusters. The ship zoomed along in the viper-ship's trail, through the space-carnage.